www.mascotbooks.com

The REAL Story of Little Red Riding Hood

For more information, please contact:
Mascot Books
620 Herndon Parkway, Suite 320
Herndon, VA 20170
info@mascotbooks.com

Library of Congress Control Number: 2020914030

CPSIA Code: PRT1120A
ISBN-13:978-1-64543-657-7

Printed in the United States

The REAL Story of Little Red Riding hood

Joe Bunting

Illustrated by
Alejandro Echavez

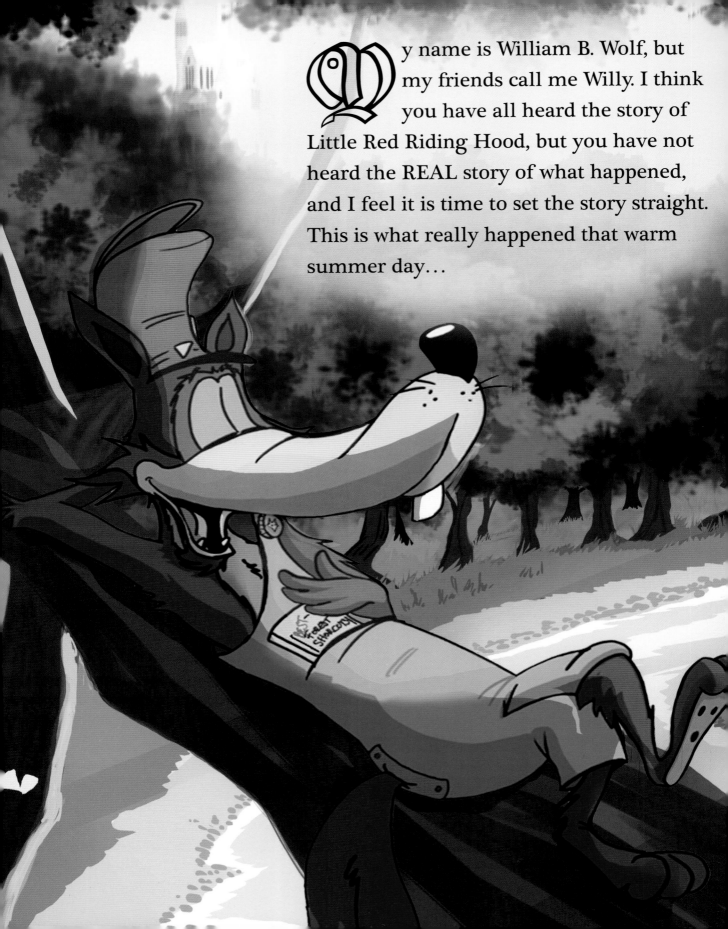

My name is William B. Wolf, but my friends call me Willy. I think you have all heard the story of Little Red Riding Hood, but you have not heard the REAL story of what happened, and I feel it is time to set the story straight. This is what really happened that warm summer day…

Nestled in a little cottage by the river lived a mother and her daughter, Little Red Riding Hood. One July afternoon, her mother put together a care basket of sweet treats and fresh warm bread and instructed her daughter to take the basket to her sick grandmother who lived just outside the Dark Forest. After much convincing, Little Red Riding Hood finally agreed to take the care basket to her grandmother, and off she went.

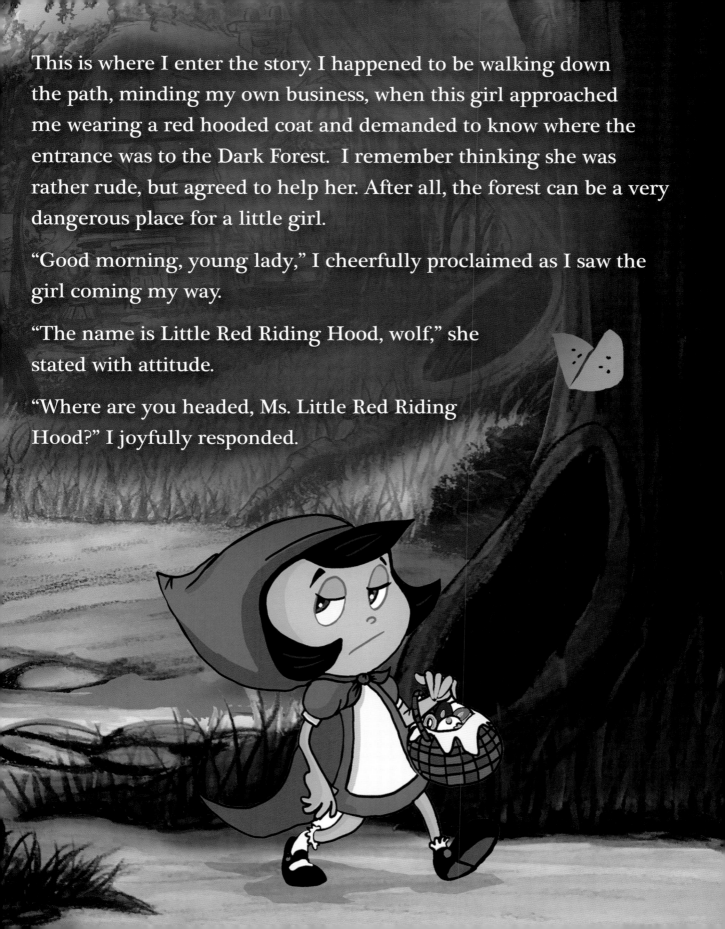

This is where I enter the story. I happened to be walking down the path, minding my own business, when this girl approached me wearing a red hooded coat and demanded to know where the entrance was to the Dark Forest. I remember thinking she was rather rude, but agreed to help her. After all, the forest can be a very dangerous place for a little girl.

"Good morning, young lady," I cheerfully proclaimed as I saw the girl coming my way.

"The name is Little Red Riding Hood, wolf," she stated with attitude.

"Where are you headed, Ms. Little Red Riding Hood?" I joyfully responded.

"To my grandmother's house. My mom says she is really sick and might not be alive much longer."

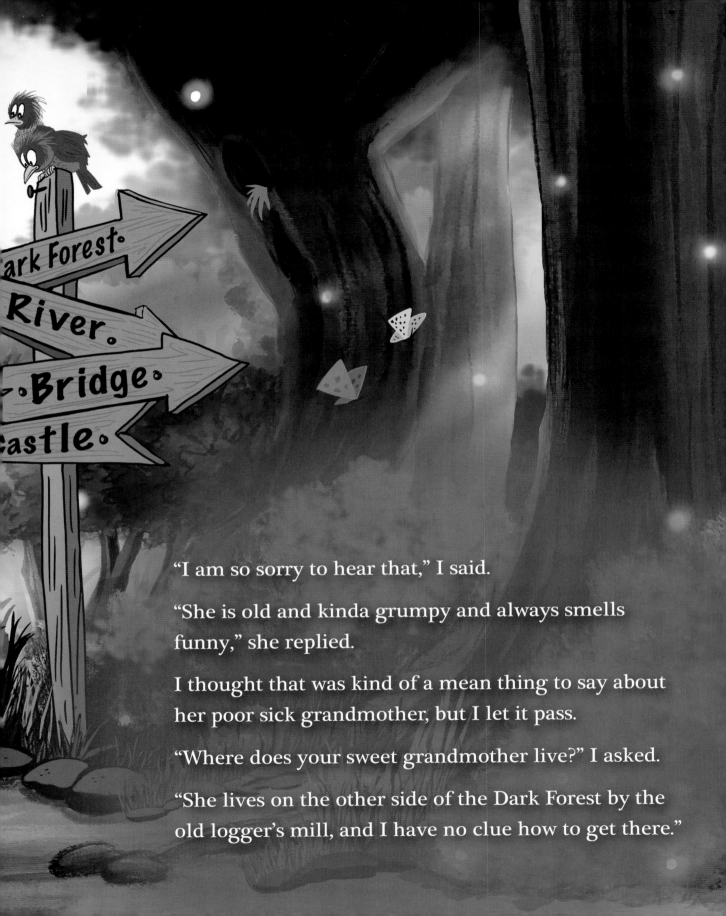

"I am so sorry to hear that," I said.

"She is old and kinda grumpy and always smells funny," she replied.

I thought that was kind of a mean thing to say about her poor sick grandmother, but I let it pass.

"Where does your sweet grandmother live?" I asked.

"She lives on the other side of the Dark Forest by the old logger's mill, and I have no clue how to get there."

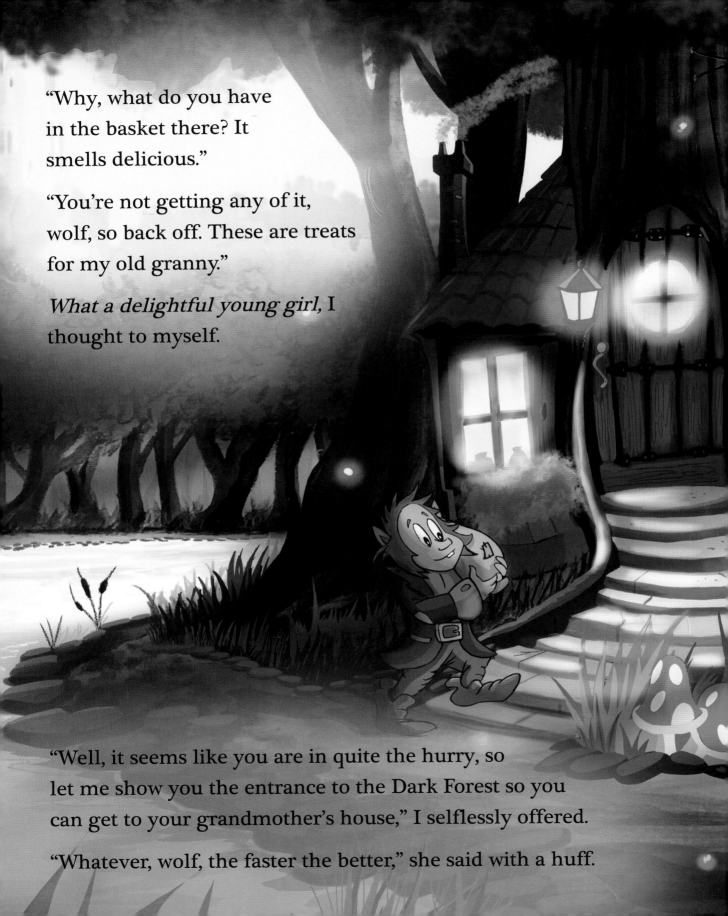

"Why, what do you have in the basket there? It smells delicious."

"You're not getting any of it, wolf, so back off. These are treats for my old granny."

What a delightful young girl, I thought to myself.

"Well, it seems like you are in quite the hurry, so let me show you the entrance to the Dark Forest so you can get to your grandmother's house," I selflessly offered.

"Whatever, wolf, the faster the better," she said with a huff.

On down the path, we walked together as she continued to complain about the distance and the fact that her shoes were getting dirty. With each step I realized how ungrateful and spoiled Little Red Riding Hood was.

As we got to the entrance of the Dark Forest, I suggested that she pick some of the wild daisies that grow along the path to give to her grandmother as a gift when she arrived. After rolling her eyes, she shrugged and said she might pick some up.

After Little Red Riding Hood scuffled down the path, I started thinking, *This poor grandmother is there all alone and about to be visited by her mean, ungrateful little granddaughter who obviously doesn't even like her. So,* I thought, *maybe it would be a nice gesture if I went ahead myself and paid her a little visit.*

Knowing a shortcut through the forest, I set off to get to the cottage ahead of the snotty Little Red Riding Hood so that her poor grandmother would at least have a pleasant visitor.

Upon arriving at her cottage, I noticed the most unusual signs everywhere indicating that visitors were not welcome. What kind of a person refuses to have friendly visitors? Thinking this must be a mistake, I went ahead and knocked on the door.

STAY OUT

KEEP OUT

DO NOT ENTER

"Who is it? Didn't you see the signs?!" shouted a voice from inside the house.

"Hello, Grandmother! This is Willy the Wolf. I just ran into your granddaughter on the road and she said you were feeling sick."

Kee
Ou

NO TRESPASSING

GO BACK

GO AWAY

DONT COME IN

STAY AWAY

GO BACK

"I can't hear you!" she shouted. "What do you want?"

Naturally, I went inside so she could hear me more clearly.

That is when she started to rudely yell at me for coming into her house to pay her a visit. What kind of ungrateful, rude family was this? Here I was, paying this poor grandmother a visit, and all she could do was demand that I leave. Can you believe that?

That's when I started to think, *She is already pretty sick and will probably suffer over the next few weeks until she eventually dies. Not to mention, she is already pretty old and has lived a very long life.* So . . . I figured, why not eat the old grandmother and put her out of her misery? Not to mention how rude she was! I would be doing her and probably all her neighbors a huge favor by eating her. So, of course, I had to eat little sick grandmother.

That's when I remembered that Little Red Riding Hood was on her way to the house, and I did not want her to be disappointed that her grandmother wasn't there to taste her basket of delicious treats.

So, I did what anyone would do . . . I dressed up as her grandmother, got in the bed, and pretended to be asleep. I was hoping that she would just let me stay fake asleep when she arrived, but just as I suspected, she rudely shouted she was there when she arrived, which would have woken any sleeping soul.

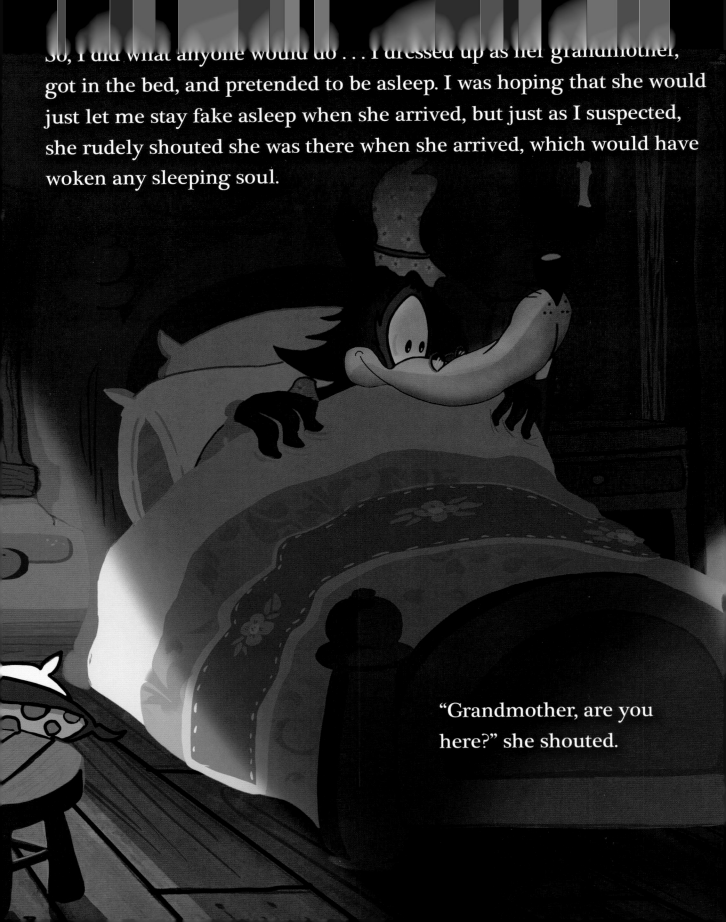

"Grandmother, are you here?" she shouted.

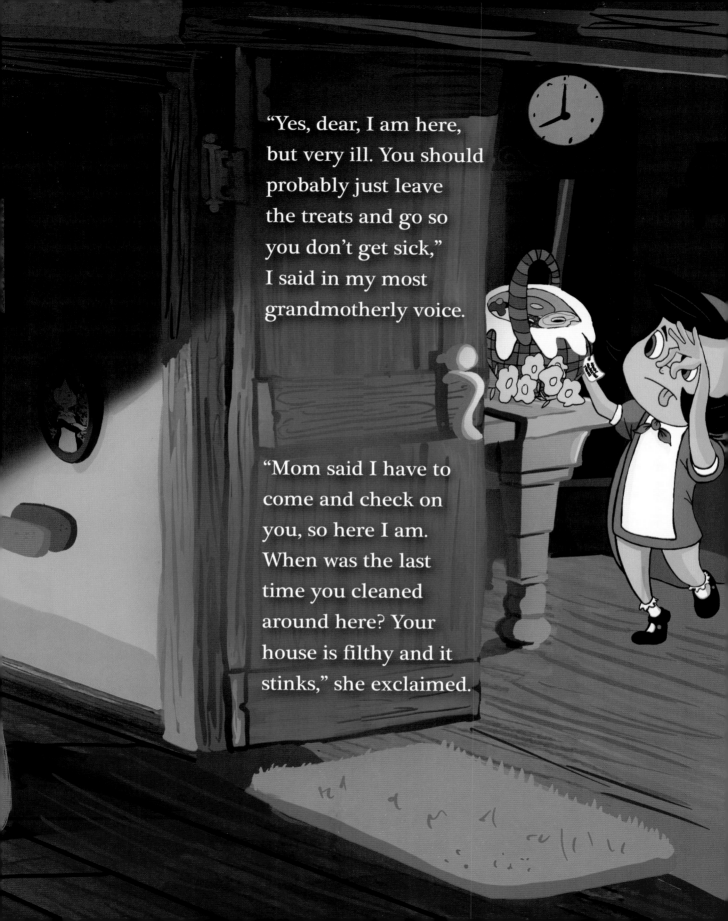

"Yes, dear, I am here, but very ill. You should probably just leave the treats and go so you don't get sick," I said in my most grandmotherly voice.

"Mom said I have to come and check on you, so here I am. When was the last time you cleaned around here? Your house is filthy and it stinks," she exclaimed.

This girl is really a piece of work, I thought. How lucky for her grandmother that I had just eaten her, so she didn't have to hear all these rude comments.

"Oh deary, I have been so sick lately. I just haven't had time."

"Whatever, it's gross," I could hear her mumble. "I am coming in, Grandmother, so put your robe on this time," she shouted from the other side of the door.

And as she entered, I pulled the covers up and asked her not to turn the lights on, as they would hurt my eyes.

As she got closer, she leaned in and said, "Why Grandmother, what big ears you have!"

"The better to hear you with my dear," I answered.

Then she leaned in even closer and said, "Why Grandmother, what big eyes you have!"

"The better to see you with my dear," I replied in a high grandmotherly voice.

That's when she leaned in all the way and said, "Why Grandmother, what big teeth you have!"

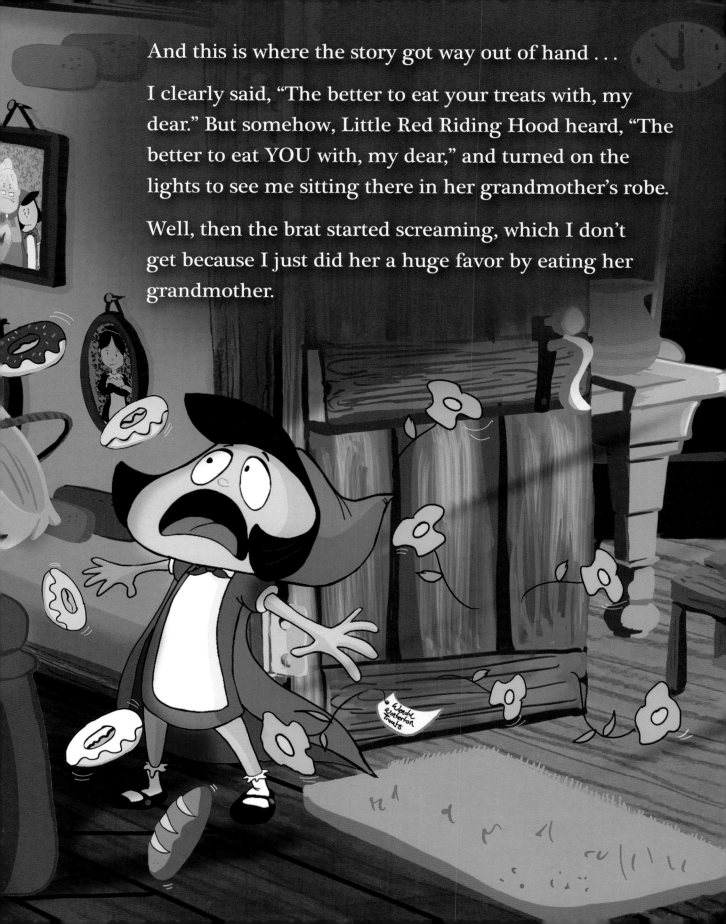

And this is where the story got way out of hand . . .

I clearly said, "The better to eat your treats with, my dear." But somehow, Little Red Riding Hood heard, "The better to eat YOU with, my dear," and turned on the lights to see me sitting there in her grandmother's robe.

Well, then the brat started screaming, which I don't get because I just did her a huge favor by eating her grandmother.

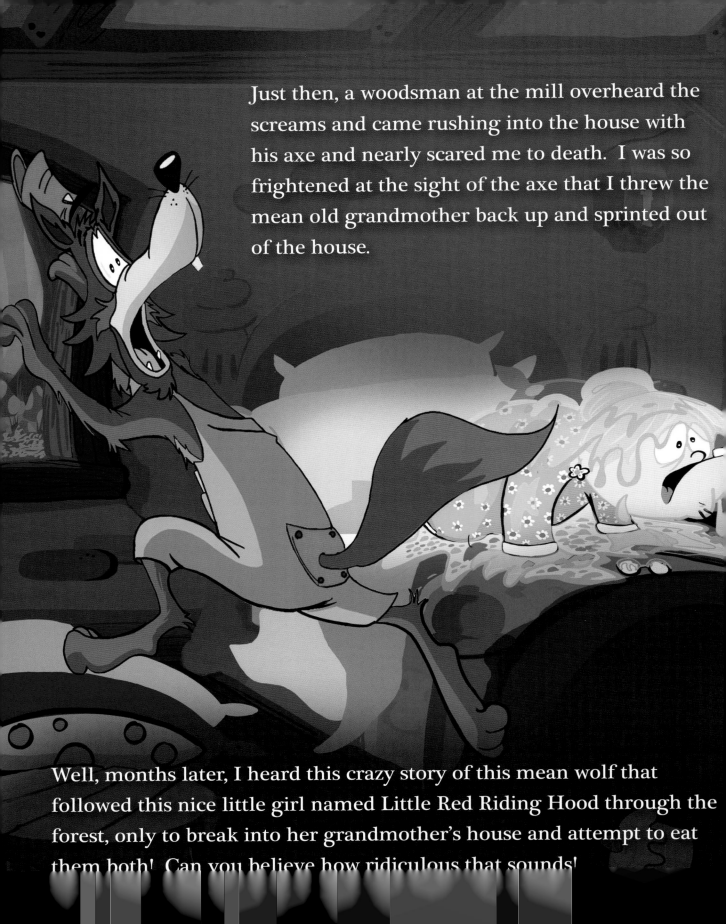

Just then, a woodsman at the mill overheard the screams and came rushing into the house with his axe and nearly scared me to death. I was so frightened at the sight of the axe that I threw the mean old grandmother back up and sprinted out of the house.

Well, months later, I heard this crazy story of this mean wolf that followed this nice little girl named Little Red Riding Hood through the forest, only to break into her grandmother's house and attempt to eat them both! Can you believe how ridiculous that sounds!

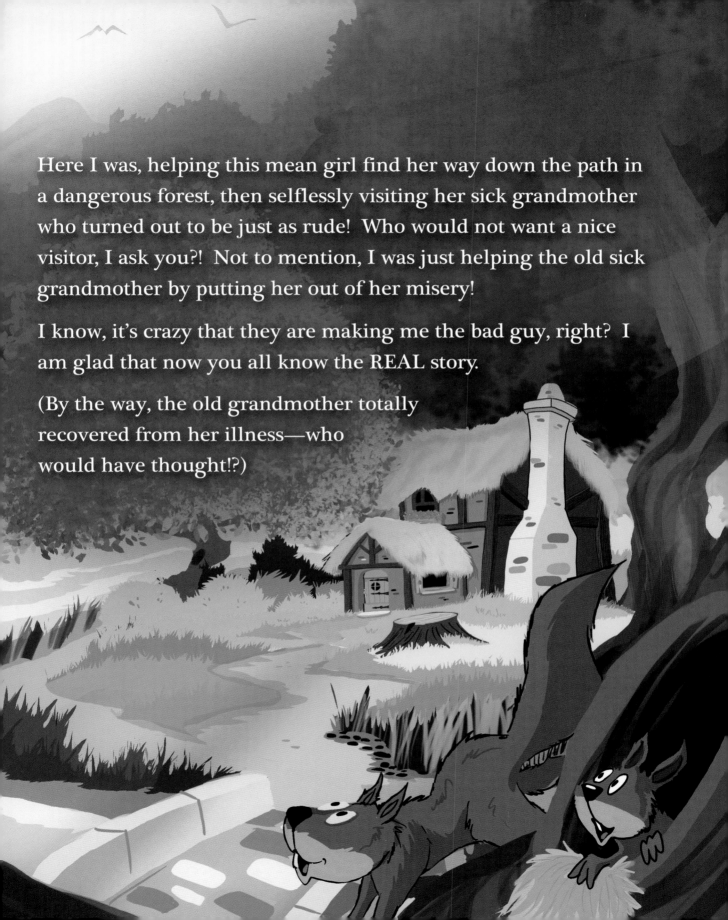

Here I was, helping this mean girl find her way down the path in a dangerous forest, then selflessly visiting her sick grandmother who turned out to be just as rude! Who would not want a nice visitor, I ask you?! Not to mention, I was just helping the old sick grandmother by putting her out of her misery!

I know, it's crazy that they are making me the bad guy, right? I am glad that now you all know the REAL story.

(By the way, the old grandmother totally recovered from her illness—who would have thought!?)

The REAL
End

Untold Classics

Old Tower

Castle

Town

Wind Mill

Red Riding Hood's House

Hansel & Gretel Home

Water Mill

Rumpelstiltskin's Home

Goldilocks Home

Wendy Winterton's
Home

Grandma's
House

Three Bears
Home

Enchanted
Forest

Dark
Forest

Old Bridge

N
W E
S

Logging
Mill

✓ Did you spot these in the story?

- ⬡ Wendy Winterton's home
- ⬡ A curious owl
- ⬡ A deer
- ⬡ A family portrait
- ⬡ Rumpelstiltskin
- ⬡ A blue butterfly
- ⬡ The castle
- ⬡ The Bear's home
- ⬡ A purple bird
- ⬡ Hansel and Gretel's home

About the Author

Joe Bunting, the renowned author of the UntoldClassics children's book series, featuring titles like *The REAL Story of Rumpelstiltskin, The REAL Story of Hansel and Gretel,* and *The REAL Story of Goldilocks and the Three Bears,* brings you another amazing untold classic with Little Red Riding Hood.

As a father of two, Joe started writing stories to entertain and captivate his young children at bedtime, which evolved into a series of hilarious untold classic tales. Joe has a unique skill for transforming classic tales and twisting your perspective of what really happened. You never know where the story will lead, but always enjoy the ride.